RAJA BETA

ARUN KUMAR JAIN

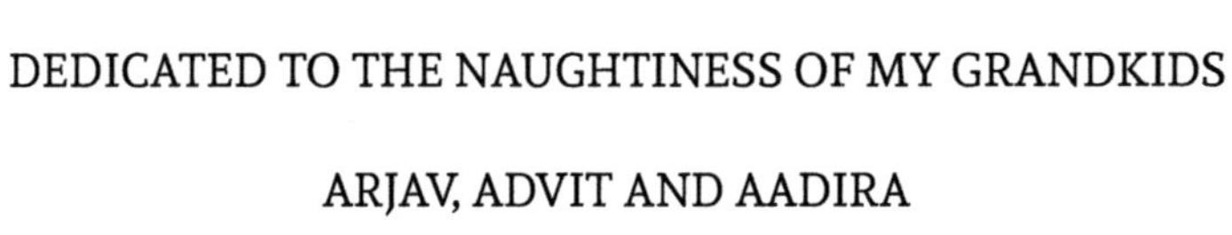

DEDICATED TO THE NAUGHTINESS OF MY GRANDKIDS

ARJAV, ADVIT AND AADIRA

Contents

Preface

In 1985, my younger brother Sri Ajay Jain started a school in our ancestral village, Dailwara (Lalitpur, U.P), in the memory of my father Late Shri Babulal Ji and grandfather Sri Jwala Prasad Ji. This school has been providing education to 250 children every year upto eighth standard since last 25 years. Our school is one of the best schools in the district. I too got several opportunities of meeting these students. Inspite of want of facilities students are excited for best performance to make their future bright. I got the source of my children's novel from these children and finally gave shape to this novel.

This story is inspiring for all of us too along with the children. Whenever we are trapped in deep moments of disappointment and depression, characters like Dinesh, enlighten our mind with hope destroying the cover of disappointment.

I want to dedicate this children's novel to all those youngsters who ruin their future, being misguided, surrounded by depression. This creation of mine will give them some keys that will open their depressed mind and provide them their desired goals.

Most Respected dynamic and active, dedicated to misson of AmmA Mata Amritanandmayi Devi Shri Satyanand ji Mishra, IAS (Retd.) , Ex-Chief Information Secterty of Government of India has made my novel more meningful by writing it's preface. I am also thankful to Dr Dinesh Pathak, Mathura and Smt. Vandana Asthana for translating it into English.

After 'Pratiksha', 'Bhakti Prasoon', 'Pathreela Yatharth' 'Sanjog, RAJA BETA, LORI THITHOLI, this is my seventh book, first in English RAJA BETA,composition dedicated to children and adolescents of the country. Very soon my dear children will be gifted witth another poetry book in Hindi NANHI CHIRIYA '. It will provide a new path to my young children who are badly trapped in the fatal games of mobile and T.V and give them a bright future.

ARUN KUMAR JAIN

#16,VENUS MEENAKSHI PLANET CITY, BAGH MUGALIA, BHOPAL, MP

#B6/303,RPS SAVANA, SECTOR 88, FARIDABAD, HARIYANA, 121009

MAIL ID, arun.k. jain23@gmail.com

Mobile #7999469175

RAJA BETA

ONE

RAJA BETA

==============

It was the Annual function of school. The whole campus was decorated interestingly. All the students were to be awarded the prizes of their achievements of the whole year. Every face was lit up with enthusiasm and excitement. Parents had also come along with their children to enjoy the programme. These were pleasant and enjoyable moments for them too. And why not, their children were to be awarded moving a step ahead in the direction of fulfilling their dreams. The function was formally inaugurated. After cultural programmes like- songs, dance, one-act plays and many other presentations, meritorious students were called on the stage. Suddenly there was an announcement- "Master Dinesh Singhai is called on the stage to receive, School's best student Award of the year, who is not only in the merit list of board exams, but he has also excelled in games, creative activities and different projects in the school. He is the most disciplined and enthusiastic student of the school. We also invite his parents- Mr. Arihant Sanghai and Mrs. Kiran Sanghai, whose efforts and encouragement has made Dinesh a versatile personality."

Dinesh with his parents came on stage. Having received the Honour, Certificate and Momento from the chief guest, his parents felt honoured and loved him. Dinesh was handed the mike to reveal the secret of his success.

"Honourable guests present in the campus, respected teachers, my parents and my dear friends. Secret of my success is my mother,

her strength and her blessings! Whenever I was disappointed and depressed at the time of difficulty, she always advised me to have patience and courage. She always said, “Only a coward fears the danger. You are my good boy ‘Raja Beta’. You are Dinesh who gives light and energy to the whole world.” I am progressing on this ideal. Salute to you maa.”

The whole pandal reverberate with thunderous applause. The whole audience gave a big hand to his mother with clapping. Everyone’s eyes were wet. Tears flowed from eyes of many mothers, while many children were looking at their mothers proudly.

Tears came in Dinesh’s eyes too and he was lost in past, where he could see his mother blessing him and smiling.

Mother, yes Dinesh’s mother, Shyama who gave life, breath, inspiration with hard work because of which he was standing proudly among the honourable persons. He could clearly see his childhood as a movie.

His mother Shyama was on death bed. She was unconscious. Dinesh was in a dilemma due to anxiety and sorrow. He had bought medicines for mother with the few rupees left in house. But there was no improvement in her condition. It was getting worse. She called groaning in pain, "Dinesh.... Dinesh........."

“What happened maa!” He spoke with a clogged throat.

“Now I am leaving, my dear.” Sharda said breaking down.

“Don’t say so, mother ! You will recover.” He too broke down.

“No dear, not anymore, I am leaving.” Shyama’s voice was fainting, Dinesh was terrified. He was unable to understand, what to do and started weeping bitterly.

“Come here, Dinesh.” Mother called again.Dinesh went near Shyama. She put her hand on his head and her hand dropped down and her head tumbled in one direction.

“MOTHER.... , MOTHER...!" he cried but she had departed from this world. Everything was hazy before him. The hut seemed to haunt him.

“No, mother! how can you leave me like this.” He clinged to the dead body of his mother and wept bitterly. People from neighbourhood came and collectively they conducted the funeral ceremony.

Many of them consoled him and promised to support him. But gradually all the consolations and promises disappeared. It was very difficult for people in such poor locality to get two square meal a day and so it was in vain for Dinesh to expect help from them.

Dinesh was completely alone as if fallen in deep well. There was neither life nor light. He was very sad. His eyes were red and swollen due to persistent weeping. He had been feeling hungry, suffocated and helpless in the lonely house. He came out of the cell and moved towards bazaar. There were many shops of eatables. Market of small town, bus stop, market place, everything was in the small area. Being hungry for two days, Dinesh felt greedy to eat. But he had no money, what should he do?

"Steal?"

"No"

"Then what he could do?"

"No, he would not steal." He decided firmly.

Suddenly his eyes fell on a stopping bus. Some youngboys were running in the same direction and when the bus stopped, they started shouting, "Coolie!, Coolie!" He also reached there immediately. A lady got down from the bus. She had a very heavy suitcase in her hand. Many boys rushed towards her. Dinesh also reached there. Those boys started approaching her to carry her suitcase. The lady saw that a boy was looking st the suitcase silently. The lady saw the boy and asked him to carry her bag. A smile came on Dinesh's face. He lifted the heavy suitcase with his small hands and keeping it on his head, followed her. Walking some distance the lady sat in a auto rikshaw and gave Dinesh five rupees. Those five rupees seemed five hundred to Dinesh. He forgot his hunger and continued for the same work and earned 25 Rs. within 2-3 hours. Now he was feeling very hungry. He moved ahead and saw some children selling gram, peas and groundnut in a tin box hung in their neck. He bought some grams for 10 Rs. and started eating it, sitting on the platform. The gram tasted better than costly sweets to his empty stomach. He ate some of the grams and moved towards his hut with the remaining. On the way he thought about his future and decided he would also sell gram. Next three days he did the work of porter.

Then he went to the grocery shop. He bought gram and salt with the remaining money and came to his cell. Reaching home he felt very sad and remembered his mother. he wept bitterly.

"Maa, why did you leave me? How shall I live now? To whom will I talk? Who will feed me lovingly?"

But then he thought that he will do. He consoled his heart, took off his clothes and sat down. He caught sight of a box of glass in the room which was empty. He took that box, cleaned it and kept the roasted gram inside it. He tore some pages from an old notebook and made some packets of gram. He made twenty packets and slept. There was a peace in his mind while sleeping.

The sun had come high up in the sky when he got up in the morning. He got up, washed his face and took a bath under a tap on road, filled the drinking water, cleaned his small room and ate the leftover food of evening. He hung that glass box in his neck and moved towards the bus stand. Boys laughed at him but he kept walking silently. He had to work hard to fill his belly. Reaching the bus stop he started shouting his wares- Gram, fresh gram, mixture.... People around started buying gram. Within 2-3 hours all his grams were sold. He had earned 100 Rs. Then he went to grocery shop and purchased some roasted gram , and groundnut and some flour and potatoes. Coming home he kneaded some flour. It was first time so the flour became loose, he kept on adding flour and water again and finally the dough was prepared. His hand was stained with wet flour. Then he put fire in the hearth. Tears flowed from his eyes due to smoke. He remembered his mother and thought that if his mother were alive, she would have fed him lovingly. He felt very miserable but he kept pan on the hearth and prepared the chapati. His hands got burnt as he was too small and unaccustomed to do this work. Anyhow he could prepare the chapatis, some got burnt while some others remained unbaked. Remembering his mother, he started sobbing and then a flood of tears started flowing from his eyes. Then he controlled himself and ate his food with potato mash.

He was very tired till then, so he laid down on the ground and slept there only. When he woke up, it was 4 o'clock. Hotness of the day had decreased and cool air had started blowing outside. He became ready and went to sell his gram and groundnut. This became his daily routine. Getting up early in the morning, having a bath, cleaning house, becoming ready and going out to sell groundnut, cooking and sleeping. At night he used to eat the lunch only. after sometime he learnt to do all work. He saved some money also. Parvati dadi, in the neighbourhood, guided him in some of his works. She was well-wisher of his mother Shyama.

One day when Dinesh was going to market, the mischievous boy of his locality, Ramu saw him. He told his friends, "See, Deenu looks happy these days, let's trouble him today."

Some of the boys agreed with him, while some others didn't. They had sympathy with him due to his miserable condition. But all were helpless before Ramu.

Dinesh never locked his room. Ramu saw no one in the street. He immediately opened the door of his room and all the boys entered and started ransacking everything in the room. Ramu got the bag which contained the money earned by Dinesh. He took out all the money, filled the bag with stones and ran away from there immediately. All the other boys also ran behind him. They all went to hotel and ate sweets there. Some money was still left. Ramu claimed that he had found out the money so he deserves, rest of the money.

But the other boys wanted that it should be distributed among all. Quarrel started. A constable was passing from there. He caught hand of Ramu. When other boys tried to run away from there, the constable, rebuked and abused them. They could not run away from there. The policeman cried, "Hey! Why are you all fighting?" All the children were taken aback and started trembling. None of them opened his mouth. He slapped Ramu. Ramu got very nervous. Soon there was a big crowd. Dinesh was returning from the market. He too came there, Ramu grew more nervous when he saw Dinesh. The constable took a search and got 95 Rs. in Ramu's pocket. Now Ramu was afraid that he would be badly beaten. He immediately made a new plan and he said, "All these boys had brought some money from their houses and deposited with him, with a plan that they would go somewhere to eat something. Sallu said that he would like to eat mixture, Shyamu demanded Rasgulla, Kullu demanded milk cake. All started quarrelling among themselves.

The policeman asked strictly, "Is this true?" Boys thought that if they spoke the truth the policeman would beat them and Dinesh would also complain in their houses. Hence, they all consented to what Ramu had said.

"Oh! You all steal money from your houses. Parents earn with such a great difficulty and you all waste their money." He took all the boys to police station. There, they were beaten badly and their money was also snatched.

When they came out from the police station, the passer by were laughing at them. They moved with their head down feeling ashamed. Walking slowly, when they reached a lane, Kallu said slowly, "Ramu got us punished!"

Ramu got angry and cried, "What are you saying? I got you punished!"

All said in a chorus, "Yes only you had told us to go to Dinesh's house and steal money from there."

Ramu said, "Didn't you all eat sweets?"

"Beating was much more painful than the taste of sweets" Sallu said.

Ramu said angrily, "You want some more beating?" all were afraid, so went away to their houses silently.

When Dinesh was coming home, he met Ramu's father. He was a gentleman. He informed him about the incident. He punished all the boys after reaching home.

When Dinesh reached home, he found everything disturbed. All the things in the room were lying in a haphazard way. When he picked up his money bag, he found it heavier. Opening it, he found that there were pebbles inside it and the money was missing. He felt the whole room revolving, but he understood everything. He could understand that it was the work of Ramu, Sallu and Kallu. He recalled that, in the morning when he was going, he had met Ramu. He had frowned at Dinesh and there was a sense of mischief on his face.

Dinesh became very upset. All his hard work and earning went in vain. A deep cry came out from his heart and his mind said, "Oh God! If you want to give me so much pain then why don't you take away my life? Why are you tormenting me? Take away my life too as you took away mother's life." He wept bitterly. Tears flowed from his eyes.

Tears of this young boy were heart breaking, but it's the irony of his fate that all this was not on the rainbow coloured screen of theatre. This cry was in the hut of a poor boy, let alone feeling his pain, there was no one to hear his heart-breaking cry.

Sad Dinesh laid on his cot, empty stomach and sank into sleep after some time. He dreamt in his sleep-

"Oh maa! U have come!"

"Yes dear, I have come."

"I knew mother u would certainly come. You can't see your Deenu sad."

"Mother, see how much troubled I am! I have grown so weak maa!"

"Yes dear, you have grown very weak."

Lovingly she hugged Dinesh, with a smile on her face.

"Without you I feel very lonely and sad, mother I always thought that I am alone in this world. That's why I have grown so weak, mother"

He sobbed and tears flowed from his eyes.

"No dear, you must have courage and patience in the time of difficulty. Cowards flee from danger, not brave. You are my brave boy, my Raja Beta. Never fear from troubles. Always remember, result of patience and hard work is always sweet."

Mother's affectionate words echoed in the room.

Deenu agreed to his mother.

"No mother, I will not cry any more. But mother you also do not leave me. I am too young for these pains. And there is no one to support me except you."

Dinesh sobbed in his mother's embrace. Laying iln her lap, he felt a boundless peace, pleasure and satisfaction. Tears of love were flowing from mother's eyes. All his troubles, worries and disappointment were washed away with these tears.

Dinesh woke up suddenly, feeling his bed wet. The bedsheet was wet with his tears. He trembled seeing noone around him.

"Mother! where did you go? I am alone. You left me again, mother!" his cry echoed in the room.

Then he realised that he was dreaming. Once again he felt lonely. Helpless and painful tears started flowing again from his eyes. Suddenly mother's voice echoed in his ears.

"No, my son! You must keep patience and courage in the times of difficulty. Cowards fear difficulty. Are you not my 'Raja Beta' good boy?"

"No, mother I need your support." He sobbed bitterly.

"My support is always with you dear. I am always with you. You are my good boy. Promise me? You will never be disappointed." He could again hear inspiring words of his mother.

"I am always with you." He thought that his mother and God both are supporting him to move ahead.

"Mother, I will never be nervous in future. I am your Raja Beta, Maa ! " Dinesh murmured.

Darkness of the night could no more be seen in the redness of dawn . Light बेटा his mother's blessings dispersed the darkness of disappointment. Dinesh got up from his cot. Despite being hungry , there was a new excitement within him. A determined smile flickered across his lips . Quickly he got ready. A new determination was taking birth in his mind .

He had only one day's earning in his pocket . He reached market, took breakfast in a small shop. Suddenly his eyes caught sight of a column in a newspaper " 20,000 rupees ! My son , Ajay , age – 10 years, is missing . The person searching Ajay will be rewarded with 20,000 rupees along with the travelling allowance and below this announcement there was a short note –

"Dear Ajay, come back where ever you are . Your mother is very sad. We shall take care of all your wishes . Nobody will say anything ."

- Your father

And beside the note there was Ajay's photograph , his father's address and his phone number.

He smiled seeing the advertisement . How colourful the world is! He thought , how unlucky he is , who never got the opportunity to see face of his father and now he has lost his mother also .

On the other hand such sons who leave their houses due their stubbornness . He felt like laughing at the strangeness of this world. Still he noted down the phone number of Ajay's father. He again went to the bus stop and started the same work of coolie. Because today he had no money. Now Deenu had turned smarter, hence very soon he was able to earn 50 rupees . After being tired he came back . As per his usual routine , he purchased some flour , potato , onion and with the remaining money he bought some gram and came to his room . As usual he cooked food , ate and made packets of gram .

Today when Deenu was returning , he was sadly thinking of the meagre money he could earn and if this money is lost he would again be bankrupt . Suddenly an idea struck his mind and he became eager to fulfil it .

He took a trolly on rent and kept groundnuts, gram , toffee and snacks and started to sell . Due to his hard work of the last few days he was able to buy so many things .

Today he earned 300 rupees . His joy knew no bounds . Now instead of saving money , he was focused on enlarging his business . With all the 300 rupees he purchased many things and came back home .

Now it was one month and Dinesh was able to buy his own trolly . He earned more money than before.

One fateful day, he was pushing his trolly, singing a song when suddenly , on a turn , the front wheel of his trolly got hit by truck and Dinesh was thrown away . All things on the trolly got scattered and Dinesh was unconscious . The truck driver drove away his truck .

A crowd gathered there . People felt sympathy for him . They helped him to get up . He was not much wounded , so he came to senses . After coming to senses, he recalled the accident with the truck and immediately ran to find his trolly . As soon as he saw his destroyed trolly , tears flowed from his helpless eyes. His heart cried . Tears flowed from his eyes persistently . He lost his patience . He started blaming God .

"Oh God ! Is this your justice? I worked so hard . Stayed awake the whole night ! Starved ! I earned honestly . But what did you give me ? Tears ! Pain ! Sorrow ! Helplessness ! Is this your justice? Is this the truth? " Dinesh cried .

"People who are dishonest , do nasty work , disintegrate the society, flee from work , commit crimes, get all the pleasure and wealth and we cannot even die in peace . Why ? Why God ? Why is there so injustice in the society ! You are God of justice ! You are kind ! But can't you see my sorrow?" Saying this Dinesh burst into tears and started walking disappointedly and aimlessly .

He felt depressed , body felt weak , he kept walking , he was suddenly shocked . A river was flowing in front of him and there was no way ahead. He thought of ending his life in the river. The problem will come to end. He started to make his resolution firm. As soon as he moved a step ahead, his mother's voice spoke, "You are my Raja Beta! Promise me you will never get disappointed. I am always with you."

He could see smiling face of his mother, inspiring to struggle.

"I am very tired mother! life's darkness does anot allow me to progress. I have neither you nor father, neither brother or sister, how can I move in life!"

"When I will die, at least I will get shade of your affection." Dinesh said crying.

"No dear, there is always a bright morning after the dark night, smiling affectionately and full of God's blessings and mother's grace. Wait for that morning my son!"

These were his mother's inspiring words.

"And listen dear, my blessings and love are always with you, even now you just have to feel it. Your name is 'Dinesh' it means 'To give light to the world'. Dinesh remove the darkness, be hopeful, enthusiastic and full of spirit my son!".

Once again Dinesh took his steps back and a desire to live amidst struggles awoke in his heart.

"Ok mother! I shall struggle till the last drop of my blood. I will be support for others, and show them the way. I am your Dinesh, maa!" His eyes became wet and he sat by the side of river in the silence of the night. He forgot his hunger, tension and sorrow. Once again he was filled with the light of hope. He was lost in the cool breeze coming from the river and fell sleep.

After sometime, when he awoke, he saw a small child sleeping at some distance. He went near him and was shocked to see that the boy was unconscious. Dinesh felt pity to see the miserable condition of the boy. He splashed some water on his face and massaged his legs and feet. Slowly the boy was coming to senses.

"Where am I?" There was a sense of fear on his face. "Don't worry, I am Dinesh. I live nearby. What happened? What is your name?" He asked many questions at a time.

Dinesh was happy to help him. Many thoughts were coming to his mind. " May be he is an orphan like me. Both of us will work hard and live together."

"What happened? Why don't you speak?" his face still revealed a sense of fear.

"I have run away from my house. My name is Ajay. Wandering many days, I jumped into the river to end my life. But I don't know how I was saved. Now I don't want to go back to my house." He said sobbing.

He narrated all his story. Ajay was the same boy whose advertisement of missing, Dinesh had read in a newspaper, few days back. Whose father had declared a reward of 20,000 Rs. for this.

Ajay's mother was weeping bitterly, father was sad, but Ajay was spoilt due to being over pampered and living in the world of money. He wasted his time, did not study and when his parents scolded him due to poor result, he left his house with some money. He wandered till he had money and then decided to end his life jumping into the river. But God had other plans, so he came on the bank of the river in an unconscious state.

Dinesh consoled him. He was shocked to hear Ajay's story. He thought, he was motherless and fatherless there is no one to speak two words of love with him, but still he was prepared to struggle in his life. On the other hand, Ajay, who has all the comforts and luxuries in his life, yet he is misusing these gifts of God and ruining his life.

He brought Ajay with him and informed his parents from a PCO booth. Ajay's parents were overjoy to hear the news. They asked Dinesh his address and got ready to go to his house and pick their son. Their life was once again hopeful of getting their son back when they had lost all hope of getting their son back.

Dinesh took Ajay to his hut. As Ajay was wounded, Dinesh gave him first aid, gave him food and warm milk and made him sleep on his own cot.

In his sweet and caring voice Dinesh said to Ajay, "This hut doesn't match your status but you have to spend a night in this. Your parents will come to receive you tomorrow or probably at night."

With his voice filled with graciousness and gratefulness, Ajay said, "No brother! For me this hut is my classroom for learning a new chapter of life and you are my inspiration. Your story revealed me the ocean of problems in this world and legends like you form their own way, struggling with the difficulties, never been disappointed being honest and hardworking in extreme situations. On the contrary, here I am, who never understood the value of the things and relations, I got and ran away leaving the safe shelter of my loving parents."

Ajay said, "Brother, I want to make a request to you!"

"Hey Ajay! What are you saying? Tell me what you want?"

"First you promise me. Then only I will speak"

"Oh my crazy brother! Do you think I will deny to your request?"

Hearing this statement of Ajay, a cluster of questions emerged in mind of Dinesh.

"What do I have that Ajay want from me? Neither meal nor house. What will he get from a labour?"

But coming out of his thoughts he assured Ajay and promised.

"You will also come with me to my house. Both of us will live together and play together. I do not have any brother. Will you be my elder brother?" Ajay looked hopefully at Dinesh. There was a deep love and urge in his voice.

"You are very innocent dear! I am an orphan son of a labour who can be used as servants in your society but can't be accepted as their own. You considered myself worthy, this is an honour for me." Deenu's eyes became wet.

"Come on, sleep now. It's too late."

"My parents are very nice, brother. And after all you have saved my life. You have changed the direction of my life. I will not go home without you." There was a sense of pleading and determination in Ajay's voice.

Both very tired and made preparation to sleep. Dinesh was connecting the different phases of his struggling life- Father's death, poverty, mother's illness, mother's death, his working as a coolie, hawker, his attempt to commit suicide, saviour of Ajay! Oh God! How many turns in a short span of time?" But still he was happy that he had saved Ajay's life. He had done a good deed. He slept with his hand affectionately on Ajay's forehead.

Suddenly both of them got up, hearing a knock at the door at 4 AM. Eyes and body were paining but he had to get up from his bed. Opening the door Dinesh saw a gentle man with his wife. There was an eagerness on their faces. They had reached Dinesh's house after asking many places and knocking at many houses. Their joy knew no bounds as soon as they saw their son Ajay.

"Ajay, my dear, where had you gone leaving us?" Ajay's mother embraced him. Tears were persistently flowing from his eyes. Ajay's father's eyes also became teary but he tried to control. He too kissed Ajay.

"Thank you dear, you have obliged us saving Ajay's life. Take you reward" Ajay's father handed 20 notes of 1000 to Dinesh.

Dinesh's eyes shone seeing such a great amount of money. For the first time, he had got the opportunity to touch the note of one thousand. He had never imagined of such a great amount. But the next moment, he became conscious and said, "No sir, I don't need all this. I had done only my duty. Please keep this money with you." Dinesh tried to return the money.

Ajay's father thought that perhaps he desires a greater amount. So he said, "No dear keep this money, we shall give you some more." He took out 5000 Rs. and extended towards Dinesh. It was nothing before his son's life.

"No Daddy, don't give money to Dinesh bhaiya. If you will give him money, I shall not go from here." His father was shocked to hear this. He seemed to be confused in this pleasant moment.

"What do you mean dear son? I am unable to understand the import of your words." He asked Ajay very lovingly. Ajay narrated the whole story from when he met Dinesh. Again and again his eyes became wet.

"He will go with us as my elder brother. Then only I shall be happy. Please daddy! Please Let him come with us" Ajay's parents became very emotional. Ajay's father became overwhelmed and said, "We can't even imagine such a jewel in midst of difficult circumstances even today on this earth. Your kindness can't be counted in money. Ajay has opened our eyes telling everything. I have a feeling, Ajay's leaving the house was a blessing in disguise for him. My son Ajay has improved himself and God has given us one more son."

Ajay's mother Kiran, became emotional and told Dinesh, "Look into my eyes dear. Don't you find your own mother?" Drowning into the ocean of mother's love and affection in Ajay's mother's eyes, he embraced Ajay's mother calling her "Maa".

His mother's words, "Result of courage, patience and honesty is always words." were echoing in his ears. The dawn breaking after the dark night was giving them the message of light, which is born from determination, honesty, hard work and devotion.

~•~

"Brother, where are you lost? Come on, everybody in the party is waiting for you." This was the voice of Ajay to his elder brother Dinesh.

"Yes, yes let's go Ajay, some past memories came to my mind." Kiran embraced Dinesh and said,"I know dear son. You were, are and will always be my Raja Beta."

"Fear of hardship, doesn't give the goal
It comes to one, who walks with his heart whole
Keep the flame of hope lit in the heart
Move every step ahead with courage in the heart
Thorns and hurdles should not block your way
Darkness or enemy should not frighten you away
Patience and courage should make your way
If you show this dare, the world is yours dear
Serving the society should be your aim
Happiness in the world is the goal you aim."

Printed by Libri Plureos GmbH in Hamburg, Germany